I0648721

Joseph Comyns Carr

King Arthur; a drama in a prologue and four acts

Joseph Comyns Carr

King Arthur; a drama in a prologue and four acts

ISBN/EAN: 9783337304768

Printed in Europe, USA, Canada, Australia, Japan

Cover: Foto ©Andreas Hilbeck / pixelio.de

More available books at **www.hansebooks.com**

KING ARTHUR,

A DRAMA

IN

A PROLOGUE AND FOUR ACTS,

BY

J. COMYNS CARR.

London:

MACMILLAN AND CO.,

AND NEW YORK,

1895.

DRAMATIS PERSONÆ.

KING ARTHUR . . . . MR. IRVING.
SIR LANCELOT . . . . MR. FORBES ROBERTSON.
SIR MORDRED . . . . MR. FRANK COOPER.
SIR KAY . . . . MR. TYARS.
SIR GAWAINE . . . . MR. CLARENCE HAGUE.
SIR BEDEVERE . . . . MR. FULLER MELLISH.
SIR AGRAVAINE . . . . MR. LACY.
SIR PERCIVAL . . . . MR. BUCKLEY.
SIR LAVAINE . . . . MR. JULIUS KNIGHT.
SIR DAGONET . . . . MR. HARVEY.
MERLIN . . . . MR. SYDNEY VALENTINE.
Messenger . . . . MR. BELMORE.
Gaoler . . . . MR. TABB.

GUINEVERE . . . . MISS ELLEN TERRY.
ELAINE . . . . MISS LENA ASHWELL.
MORGAN LE FAY . . . . . . MISS GENEVIEVE WARD.
CLARISSANT . . . . MISS ANNIE HUGHES.
Spirit of the Lake . . . . . . MISS MAUD MILTON.

Knights, Squires, Ladies of the Court, &c., &c.

Produced at the LYCEUM THEATRE, 12th January, 1895.

SYNOPSIS OF SCENERY.

PROLOGUE.

EXCALIBUR.

SCENE.—THE MAGIC MERE.

ACT I.

THE HOLY GRAIL.

SCENE.—THE GREAT HALL AT CAMELOT.

ACT II.

THE QUEEN'S MAYING.

SCENE.—THE WHITETHORN WOOD.

ACT III.

THE BLACK BARGE.

SCENE.—THE TOWER ABOVE THE RIVER AT CAMELOT.

ACT IV.

THE PASSING OF ARTHUR.

SCENE 1.—THE QUEEN'S PRISON AT CAMELOT.

SCENE 2.—THE GREAT HALL AT CAMELOT.

KING ARTHUR.

THE PROLOGUE.

EXCALIBUR.

SCENE :—*The magic Mere. A wide lake with a rocky path descending to the shore. As the curtain rises there is a faint glimmer on the horizon, which gradually spreads over the water to an effect of dawn.*

Chorus of Lake Spirits singing.

AWN and daytime turn to night,
Darkness wakes to morning light ;
All the uncounted hours go by
Swift as clouds across the sky,
While we maidens of the mere,
Heedless of the changing year,
Guard the sword Excalibur.
　　　[*During the concluding bars of the chorus,*
　　　ARTHUR, *accompanied by* MERLIN, *appears on the summit of the rocky path.*

Arth. What shore is this, haunted by mystic sounds
That are not earthly ?

Mer.　　　　　　'Tis no earthly shore,
Nor, till this hour, have mortal eyes beheld
These fairy sands.

Arth.　　　　　Then thou shalt go alone ;

B

For here, perchance, thy magic arts have power
To lure my soul.

Mer.   Nay, Arthur, have no fear.
A mightier power than mine had led thy feet
There where I found thee sleeping by the lake :
For whilst I watched a star fell in the sky,
And from the vacant space of Heaven there came
A voice that cried, "Awake! the hour hath struck :
Now guide him, Merlin, to that caverned home
Where dwells the sacred sword Excalibur."

Arth. What is this sword ?

Mer.   Look well, and thou shalt see.

[*As he speaks an arm rises from the Lake
holding aloft a jewelled sword set in its
scabbard, which gleams with supernatural
light.*

Chorus of Lake Spirits.

Sword, no mortal shall withstand,
Fashioned by no mortal hand,
Long we wait the hour shall bring
England's sword to England's King ;
    He shall wield Excalibur.

Mer. What think'st thou, Arthur ?

Arth.   Nay, I have no word.
Whence comes this sword ?

Mer.   Long time, ere Time began,
'Twas forged beneath the sea ; its glittering blade,
Was tempered by the waves ; sea-maidens wrought
Its jewelled scabbard, and that warrior king
Whose arm is strong to wield it in the fight,
Shall rule a kingdom that shall rule the sea.

Arth. [*Musing.*] For such a sword 'twere well to
        give the world,
With such a sword 'twere well to rule the world.
Who is this king ?

Mer.   Nay, list, and thou shalt hear.

Chorus of Lake Spirits.

Warrior knight, into thy hand,
Monarch of a mighty land
That, in unborn years, shall be
Monarch of the mightier sea;
Great Pendragon's son, to thee
    We shall yield Excalibur.
    [*The sword again slowly sinks into the Lake.*

Arth. Who is Pendragon's son?
Mer.   Thou art the man;
Pendragon's son, albeit thou know'st it not;
For at thy birth I took thee from the Court.
Deep in the woods—a flower amid the flowers—
I watched beside thee, heard thine infant tongue
First lisp responsive to the woodland birds,
And by thy cradle, swung beneath the stars,
Taught thee the wisdom that should fit a throne.
Now art thou called! Stand forth and take thy
    sword,
Whose might alone can stay these wasting wars,
Whose might alone shall bring the realm of peace.
    Arth. [*Rising.*] Then was my dream no dream; for
        while I slept
I heard the noise of battle, and I saw
The flashing of innumerable spears
Lightening the dark of Heaven; then I rose
And rode into the strife, and, where I led,
The mightiest fell before me, and men cried,
"It is the King!" Yet did I heed them not,
For in mine ears there rang a clarion voice
Which said, "Nay, stay not till the end is won!
Fight on, thine arm is mightier than theirs,
Fight on, an unborn empire claims thy sword,
Fight on, they strike for glory, thou for peace!"
Long time the battle lasted, and the end
Seemed afar off; yet at the end it came,
And, ere my arm grew weary, I could hear

A hush upon the thunder ; and the noise
And cry of war grew fainter, till it fell
To echoing silence.   Then far off I saw,
Set in a redd'ning sky of blood and fire,
A face most fair that wore an angel smile ;
And down the unending avenue of spears
It drew towards me, seeming as it came
Like a white rose leaf borne upon the tide
Of crimson war.   Whereat I knelt and said,
" I   have   fought   for   thee,   thou   hast   the   smile   of
        peace ; "
Yet answer made she none, and I awoke.
Ah, thou who know'st the secrets of the stars,
Tell me whose face I saw !—
  Mer.   Nay, ask not that.
  Arth. I   will   be   answered !   all   the   world   to
  me
Dwells in that smile.
  Mer.   Then look upon thy fate.
    [*As he speaks a vision of* GUINEVERE *appears.*
    ARTHUR *kneels.*
  Arth. Who art thou ?   Speak !
  Mer.   Listen, and thou shalt hear.
    [*At this a chorus of unseen spirits is heard.*

     Chorus.

   Fairest form of all the earth !
   Joy and sorrow at one birth ;
   Love and beauty, hope and fear,
   Wait for thee in Guinevere.

  Mer. Love and beauty, hope and fear,
     Wait for thee in Guinevere.
Thou hearest, Arthur ?
  Arth.   Nay, I do but see
A form too fair for this rough world's embrace,
Fit for a kingdom that no sword can win ;
Yet would I win thee, take thee for my Queen.
Ah, say she shall be mine !

Mer.   Fate answers thee,
Yet in that gift of beauty lurks thy doom.

Echoing Chorus.

Love and beauty, hope and fear,
    Wait for thee in Guinevere.

Arth. These fairy tongues are false, for, see, she
    bears
The emblems of the spring : all the new world
Leaps into flower about her ; and the may
Trails its white blossom round those stainless brows.
    Mer. Yet thou shouldst know full many a poisonous
        weed
Grows rank amid the blossoms of the may.

Chorus.

Love and Hate are born in May ;
Love, the bird upon the wing,
Hate, the worm devouring
All Love's flowers of yesterday,
    Wait for thee in Guinevere.
                    [*The vision fades.*

Mer. All Love's flowers of yesterday,
        Wait for thee in Guinevere.
Arth. Thou wilt not stay ! then I will seek for thee,
And through the world, if thou art of the world,
I'll find thee, crown thee, Guinevere, my Queen !

Echoing Chorus.

All Love's flowers of yesterday,
    Wait for thee in Guinevere.

Arth. And yet those mystic voices chaunt of doom !
Ah, thou whose vision spans futurity,
Hath not thy magic art all power to stay
The hand of Fate ?

Mer.   Our knowledge is not power.
Who knows the end of Life hath reached the end.
His wisdom is but Death ; while ye, who stand
Eager to thread the winding maze o' the world,
Led on by faith, do more than angels dare.
Such destiny is thine : for thy right arm
Out of this mound of earth shall raise a throne
Whose glory echoes through unacted time—
Wherefore I charge thee ask no more of fate.
The hand of doom is patient, and the sword
That flashes in the glimmering light of dawn
Falls not till night-fall : thou shalt rule thy day.
     Arth. I'll ask no more ; I do but crave my sword.
          [*The* Spirit of the Lake *appears, and at the
               same time the sword rises again from
               the Lake.*
Mer. Thy prayer is answered, she will give it thee.

               The Spirit of the Lake.

     Arthur, England's chosen lord,
     Fear not Fate, but take thy sword ;
     Thou the first whose mortal hand
     E'er hath touched that mystic brand.
     Sword and scabbard both are thine,
     Sword and scabbard both divine :
     Guard them well and use them well,
     So that aftertime shall tell
     Of thy kingdom in the sea,
     Blazoned on whose shield shall be,
     " Right and Might and Liberty."
          [ARTHUR *makes a movement toward the
               sword.*
     Yet beware ! Time's beating wing,
     Restless and untiring,
     Speeds along Time's endless way.
     Bravely thou shalt rule thy day,
     And at last, when Day is done,
     Those three Queens of Avalon,

Rulers of the night, who keep
In their charge the keys of sleep,
Far across this mystic mere
Silently thy barge shall steer,
Till thy wearied eyes have won
Endless sleep in Avalon.

Arth. He who would rule the day must greet the
    dawn.
There is no hour to lose ; give me my sword,
For, echoing through the night, I too can hear
The voice of England, like a sobbing child
That longs for day ; and, gathering in night's sky,
I see that throng of England's unborn sons,
Whose glory is her glory : prisoned souls
With faces pressed against the bars of Time,
Waiting their destined hour. Give me my sword,
That I may loose Time's bonds and set them free.
    [*The chorus is heard, and the picture is held
      till the fall of the curtain.*

Chorus.

Great Pendragon's greater son,
Arthur, ere thy race be run,
Thou shalt rule from sea to sea
England that is yet to be :
Great Pendragon's son, to thee
    Here we yield Excalibur.

ACT I.

THE HOLY GRAIL.

SCENE:—*The Great Hall at Camelot. A wide opening breast high at the back, flanked by marble columns, through which is seen a view of blue hills against a sunset sky.*

SIR KAY, SIR AGRAVAINE, *and* SIR BEDEVERE, *to whom enters* SIR LANCELOT.

Kay.

IR LANCELOT, this falls well: of late our King
    Hath ofttimes asked for thee, and thou shalt learn
The noise of thy great deeds hath far outstripped
Thy good steed's swiftest course, waiting thee here
To swell love's welcome home. What news from
    Wales?
  Lan. In Wales men speak in whispers; yet 'tis
    known
That Ryons, lately joined in secret league
With Mark of Cornwall, doth but wait the hour
To strike at Arthur's throne.
  Agra.   This news comes pat;
Not three days past, deep in the belt of wood
That circles round Caerleon's clustering towers,
Sir Gawaine's huntsmen chanced upon two spies,
Who now lie fast in chains.
  Kay.   And at this hour
The King holds council, and shall straight declare
If they may live or die.

Agra.   Should Gawaine speak
And Arthur listen they were dead ere night.
  Gaw. That is most sure.
  Lan.   Which way doth Mordred tend?
  Agra. Truth, that were hard to tell! his subtle
     tongue
Still weaves a web to catch the thought of others,
And hide his own.
  Lan.   And what then saith the King?
  Kay. He waits upon the word of Guinevere.
  Gaw. I dare be sworn this thing hath troubled him.
  Kay. What should he fear though Mark and Ryons,
     joined
With all the hosts of Cornwall and of Wales,
Knocked at our gates.
  Lan.   Nay, sirs, he knows not fear,
Whose warrior heart was bred where spears have
     grown
Thick as the river reeds. Yet in that heart
Dwells a fond nursling hope this news will slay;
For since the coming of Queen Guinevere
The sword Excalibur hath hung at rest
Within its jewelled scabbard, and he dreamed
The lust of blood was past.
  Kay.   Would that were all!
King Arthur grieves, but 'tis with graver cause.
  Lan. What cause?
  Kay.   What cause!
  Gaw.   In truth we do forget.
Sir Lancelot knows not that at vesper time
A hundred knights of Arthur's fellowship
Take a long leave of Camelot and the King.
  Lan. Bound on what quest?
  Kay.   No earthly quest is theirs
Who've ta'en a vow to seek the Holy Grail.
  Lan. To seek the Grail! Now, sirs, you mock
     at me!
For who, of mortal born, shall hope to find,
Searching through all the world, that holy cup

Charged with Christ's blood? That cup no eye hath
    seen
Since long ago to this White Isle 'twas borne
By Joseph, who had filled it at the Cross.
What Heaven hath hid no man may dare to seek,
Save by a sign from Heaven.
    Kay.   Heaven's sign hath come
In miracle and wonder : three nights past—
When all our company were sat at meat—
Above the murmur of the feast there leapt
The crack and cry of thunder, and the roof
Was cloven as with a sword : then down the hall,
Aslant upon a bar of light that gleamed
As though the sun were turned to molten gold,
Passed a white angel, bearing in her hands
The sacred vision of the cup of Christ.
    Lan. What like was it to see?
        [*During the following speech the hall darkens.*
    Kay.   That none may tell,
For, dimly veilèd in a cloth of white,
It went as it had come, unseen of all.
Yet while it passed it left, though none knew how,
The witness of its presence in men's eyes ;
And, dumbly gazing, each in other found
The stamp of some new glory ; then uprose
Our youngest knight, Sir Percival, and cried :
" Now thanks for what hath been and what shall be !
For here I vow to rest not till these eyes
Have openly beheld the cup itself ! "
And, as one note at dawn will wake the woods,
Voice after voice re-echoed Percival's,
Till, one by one, a hundred of our knights
Had joined themselves unto this holy quest.
    Lan. If this be so——
    Gaw.   Why, sir, 'twas in this hall!
    Kay. And close upon this hour.
        [*A peal of thunder is heard, followed by a
           lightning flash.*
    Lan.   What cry was that ?

Kay. Nay, see, 'tis here again.

> [*As he speaks, a slanting ray of light falls through the hall, enfolding the form of a maiden bearing the cup, from the centre of which a red light strikes like a star through the transparent veil that covers it.* SIR LANCELOT *kneels as the vision passes and disappears.*

Lan.   Ah, go not yet!
'Tis gone! and did mine eyes not vouch 'twas here,
I'd say it was a dream ; for never yet
Hath mortal vision gazed on aught so fair!
Didst thou not note how all the air was filled
With sweetest odours ?

Gaw.   So it was before.

Kay. Said we not truth ?

Lan. [*Rising.*]   Ay, and by this I know
That age of marvels, long ago foretold
By Merlin, when he built our Table Round,
Hath come at last ; and we who live to-day
Shall witness wonders great and terrible
Shaking the earth, until that happier hour
When he whom God hath chosen of us all
With mortal eyes shall pierce Heaven's mystery,
And see the Grail itself.

Gaw.   'Twas said last night,
That he alone shall win this saving grace
Whose heart stands clear of sin.

Lan.   Ay, sir, 'tis so.
And He alone who wills it so can pierce
The secrets of our hearts ! Not all may win,
Yet straining at the goal there's none can lose
The grace that comes of strife.

> [MORDRED *has entered unseen during the last speech, carrying a scroll in his hand.*

Mord.   How now, Sir Knights,
Ye do forget the hour ! Have ye not heard
That they whose names are duly here enrolled,
Bound by their vows to seek the Holy Grail,

Within a breathing space shall take their leave
Of Arthur and his Court?

Lan.   I pray you, sir,
Of your good grace add my name to the roll.

Mord. Hast thou considered well?

Lan.   My lord, I have,
And shall be ready when the list is called.

                    [*Exit* LANCELOT.

Mord. [*Half to himself.*] So Lancelot goes!

Kay.   I dare be sworn he will not,
Nay, though his oath were loudest of them all,
Yet Arthur's love will hold him.

Mord. [*Turning fiercely upon* KAY.] Who dares speak
So gross a treason 'gainst our lord the King?
In truth, Sir Kay, I thought thee worthier
Of Arthur's love.

Kay.   Nay, sir, I did but think
That Lancelot, who is worthier than us all,
Would go or stay as that same love commands.

Mord. And thou! and thou! yet think ye that the
                    King,
Who loves him best and knows him worthiest,
Would bid him break his vow? Now, hark'e, sirs:
Ye know not him ye worship, and your praise
Is but a vapour that doth hide the sun,
But ye shall know him! Nay, sirs, tarry not,
But see that all is ready for the King.

Kay. Be sure, my lord, we shall not fail the King.

                    [*Exeunt* KAY *and other* Knights.

Mord. [*Alone.*] Yea, Arthur's love would hold him,
                    but it shall not.
Lancelot shall go, and, in that vacant seat
Where now his heart sits guardian to the King,
Envenomed hate shall keep a closer watch.
Lancelot shall go.

Enter MORGAN.

      Ah! mother, thou art here.
What saith the Queen?
 Morg.   'She doth attend the council.
 Mord. And her voice?
 Morg.   Is tuned to plead for mercy.
 Mord. 'Tis well, for Arthur heeds no voice save
  hers.
These dogs whose tongues I feared will now go free.
 Morg. Then tell me, boy, what tidings did they
  bear?
 Mord. The gathered hosts of Cornwall and of Wales
Wait but my sign.
 Morg.   They shall not wait for long.
The year grows green, and May-day comes again—
Day of thy birth, and day of Arthur's doom.
 Mord. Of Arthur's doom?
 Morg.   Ay, for 'twas so foretold,
Ere yet thine eyes had opened on the world,
That he whose hand should strike at Arthur's
  heart
On May-day must be born. And thou art he,
For in thy veins an avenging poison flows,
Distilled in that dark hour when Merlin's lips
Hailed Arthur as Pendragon's rightful heir,
And left me bastard.
 Mord.   Ay, yet one thing lacks:
Think you, will Lancelot join this holy quest?
 Morg. What should you fear, though Lancelot go
  or stay?
 Mord. I fear, yet know not what—his loyal love
Twines around Arthur like a coil of steel
That turns the keenest edge. Yea, well I know
That while Sir Lancelot stays, the King is safe.
 Morg. Thou fool! the King were safer if he
  went.
 Mord. What dost thou say?

Morg.   I say what thou shouldst know :
The King doth love Sir Lancelot ?
    Mord.   Ay, too well!
    Morg. Too well, in truth, for next the King stands
        one
Who loves him more than well.
    Mord.   Not Guinevere ?
    Morg. Ay, she !
    Mord.   This is thy malice.
    Morg.   Think'st thou so ?
Trust me, 'tis true—a woman hath no wiles
To hide her secret from a woman's gaze
Whose eyes are never blindfold.   Dost forget
When the news came of Lancelot's heavy wound
How she did weep and wail ?
    Mord.   So did the King.
    Morg. Ay, truth, so did the King ; yet that's not
        all :
For later, when the happier tidings came
That, tended by Elaine, his wound was whole,
Hadst thou but seen her then !   The King made
        glad,
But Guinevere's white lips could shape no smile.
Her jealous heart was torn.
    Mord.   If this be so,
And Lancelot loves her too, then all are trapped !
    Morg. Nay, take it not from me, look for thyself.
                    [Herald's *trumpet heard without.*
But see she comes, take heed and guard thy tongue.

                Enter GUINEVERE.
    Mord. Madam, what saith the King ?
    Guin.   Hast thou not heard ?
Thy mother's prayer for mercy hath prevailed ;
The spies are pardoned.
    Mord.   Why then, 'tis to thee
They owe their right to live.
    Guin.   Nay, to the King !
Who knowing naught of fear, fears naught to spare

Where weaker hearts would slay.   To-day at eve
Our knights ride forth upon a Holy Quest ;
At such a season then it was not fit
That on their spotless banners there should rest
The smirch of hireling blood.

    Morg.   Madam, the King !

      Enter ARTHUR, *with* Knights *attending.*

    Arth. Our faithful knights do know th' appointed
      hour.
    Mord. My lord, they wait your call.
    Arth.   Give me the roll.
        [MORDRED *hands scroll to the* King.
Is all complete ?
    Mord.   Nay, truth, I had forgot :
One name is lacking there.
    Arth.   Whose name is that ?
Stand there not here enough of goodly knights
That I must lose from our great fellowship,
But ye would cry for more ?
    Mord.   Your pardon, Sire ;
I did but learn it now, within the hour :
Sir Lancelot hath returned.
    Arth.   Well, sir, what then ?
    Guin. [*Starting.*] Sir Lancelot home !
    Morg. [*Approaching her.*] Ay, madam, he is here.
    Arth. Lancelot is welcome home.
    Mord.   Yet 'tis to fear
He comes but to depart.
    Arth.   What mean you, sir ?
    Mord. He, too, my lord, would join this Holy
      Quest.
    Arth. Sir Lancelot? Nay, you jest! this shall not be.
Go straight and send him here.
    Mord.   My lord, I will.   [*Exit* MORDRED.
    Guin. Morgan, thou hast our leave.
    [*Exeunt* MORGAN, Ladies of the Court, *and* Knights.
              Nay, good my lord,

This troubles thee.

Arth.   It would an it were true ;
For, as each added name summed up the list,
Methought, though all should go, yet one remains ;
Flower of all knighthood, Lancelot, thou at least
Shalt stand beside thy King !

Guin.   Yet should he go
Thou still hast that which serves thee more than all,
Thy sword Excalibur, whose mystic blade
Hath carved this Island Empire from the sea,—
Thou hast thy goodly sword.

Arth.   Ay, and my Queen,
Whose dear commands are set as Heaven's high
          voice,
Lifting me nearer Heaven.

Guin.   Trust thy sword ;
'Twill serve thee better far.

Arth.   Long time gone by,
When this same sword by magic hands was given,
Old Merlin said, Take heed and guard it well ;
Yet guard the scabbard too, for that is more
E'en than the blade it sheathes.   I knew not then
If he spoke false or true : I know it now.
For at thy coming, Guinevere, my Queen,
The havoc turned to harvest at thy feet ;
From out the bellowing throat of war there came
A sweeter, softer music, and the earth,
New christened by thy smile, broke forth in flower.
Thou art our scabbard, and in thy pure soul,
Where only peace may dwell, our sword lies sheathed !
Yet that rich dower thy father gave with thee,
That image of the world, our Table Round,
A kingdom's heart set in a rim of steel
Forged of the spears of all the goodliest knights
Of all the earth ; that too must count for much,
And if he now should fail that out of all
Hath shown himself the mightiest, then I think
Our day draws to its end.

Enter LANCELOT.

                Most welcome home!
It was but now I learned from Mordred's lips
Thou too wouldst join this quest.
   Lan.   'Tis so, my lord.
   Arth. If that same word by other lips were
     spoken
I'd say 'twas false. Dost thou so lightly count
Our long-tried love, that, without word or sign,
Thou'dst quit our side? Nay, but I wrong thee
   there,
For we are one, and haply thou hast told
Thy purpose to the Queen.
   Guin.   Not so, indeed.
I heard it not till now.
   Lan.   Nay, hear me, Arthur.
I have no life, no soul that is not thine,
No heart but waits some fitting hour to bleed
In thy great cause; yet, couldst thou see that heart
And know its present sickness, thou wouldst say :
Lancelot, ride forth, thou hast our willing leave.
   Arth. Thinkest thou so? We'll speak of this again.
   Lan. Thy voice alone shall bid me go or stay.
                [*Exit* LANCELOT.
   Arth. And thou shalt stay, for now I do divine
This sickness at thy heart. [*Turning to* GUINEVERE.]
     Canst thou not guess?
   Guin. Indeed I cannot.
   Arth.   'Tis some cause of love
That bids him go.
   Guin. [*Starting.*] Of love?
   Arth.   Ay, dear, of love!
Didst think that our two hearts had drained love's
     springs?
Thou hast not heard, but, ere thy coming hither,
'Twas known that Lancelot wooed the fair Elaine.
              C

Guin. 'Twas she that nursed him when his wound
    was sore ?

Arth. Ay, true, 'twas she ; but even then their
    loves
Had drifted wide asunder, and of late
He has not breathed her name.

Guin.   Why then 'tis sure
He loves her not.

Arth.   In love there's naught that's sure.
Yet is he framed in such a constant mould
That truly I believe he loves her still.
Some little knot hath ravelled up the skein
That links their hearts.   There needs a woman's wit
To set the tangle straight.

Guin.   A woman's wit ?

Arth. Ay, dear, and thine.

Guin.   Indeed, I think not so.

Arth. Indeed 'tis so : bid Lancelot come to thee ;
Thy tongue will find a charm that may unlock
The guarded secret of his chafing heart.

                    [GUINEVERE *does not move.*
Nay, thou wilt do 't ? if our all happy love
Hath known no jar, then must we search the more
To find the missing note for those whose souls
Are not so finely tuned.

Guin.   Then thou art sure
Thou art all happy ?

Arth.   Nay, how canst thou ask ?

Guin. A little field-flower, lighted by a star,
Stands but a tiny speck beneath that lamp
Which shines o'er half the world ; yet once it dreamed
That this great beacon light was all its own.
'Tis long since thou hast spoken of thy love,
Dost know how long ?

Arth.   That is the fate of kings,
Whose lives are as a picture for the world,
Not for their own content.   When we were wed,
I dreamed of many an hour when we would sit,
Thy hand in mine, recalling that sweet day

When, like a flash of sunlight through the trees,
I saw thy face at Cameliard ; but now
The busy hours slip by, each new day brings
Its burden of new duty, and our loves
Are too long silent.   Yet full well thou know'st—
                              [*Approaching her.*
   Guin. [*Interrupting him, and making away.*] Yes,
      yes, I know ; heed not my idle words.
It was a foolish thought that slipped my tongue.
I'll do thy bidding straight.

Enter MORGAN.

   Morg. Your pardon, madam, but the fair Elaine,
Is newly come from Astolat, and craves
An audience with the Queen.
   Arth.   Now this falls well.
So you shall plead for both.
   Guin. [*To* MORGAN.]   I'll see her here.
Go tell Sir Lancelot I would speak with him.
                              [*Exit* MORGAN.
   Arth. And later, when Sir Lancelot's name is
      called,
'Tis thou shalt bid him stay.   Till then, farewell !
                              [*Exit* ARTHUR.
   Guin. Farewell !   [GUINEVERE *is left alone.*
Am I so weak that every random word
Can shake my heart ? When Arthur said but now,
" It is some cause of love bids Lancelot go,"
I trembled like a thief that's trapped at night.
For, in his god-like gaze, I thought I saw
The searching eyes of God ; piercing my soul,
Where lurks the shameful secret of my love
That none must know.   Ah me, if Lancelot knew !
How he would spurn me ! But he shall not know.
Wherefore 'twere better he should go away ;
For while he was away, within my heart

His image dwelt securely, like a star
Hung high above me in a stainless sky,—
A lamp illumined with a fireless flame
That wrought no ill,—but now, when he is by,
The light grows blinding, and its fiercer rays
Consume my very soul.

She stands wrapt in thought as enter ELAINE.

Elaine. Thy pardon, madam.   Morgan bade me
  come.
      [*She kneels as* GUINEVERE *turns to her.*
Guin. [*Aside.*] Indeed, but she is fair! [*Aloud.*]
  Nay, do not kneel.   [ELAINE *rises.*
What wouldst thou with me ?
Elaine.   'Twas but yester eve,
Within thy garden by the castle wall,
For the first time I saw thee with thy maids,
Where, 'midst them all, thy prouder beauty seemed
To wear the gentlest smile ; 'twas then I thought :
" Could I but see the Queen, I'd tell my heart
And win her favour."   Now methinks I erred.
Guin. Has, then, my face so changed ?
Elaine.   Sweet lady, no.
Yet in thy presence my poor lips are dumb.
Guin. Then I must speak for thee : sit near me here.
      [ELAINE *sits at her feet.*
So, thou art she our great Sir Lancelot loves ?
I do not wonder.
Elaine.   I did think so once.
Guin. Be sure he loves thee still.
Elaine.   Ah, would 'twere so !
Guin. Was then his love so sweet ? tell me how
  sweet.
Elaine. I scarce knew then ; for all the uncounted
  joys
Of that brief time seemed but an earnest paid
From Love's unbounded store.   Now, when all's lost,

Remembrance feeds my grief and, drowned in tears,
Brings back each little token of his love
That passed unheeded then.

    Guin.   There's joy in that—
He loved thee once; methinks I know some hearts
Would take thy sorrow's burden but to win
What thou dost still possess: but tell me more.
Such love, if love it were, could not so end
Without a cause—perchance the fault was thine.

    Elaine. I think so too, and yet I know not how.
The end came all so swiftly: on that day
When he rode forth I do remember well
I scarce was sad, our parting was so sweet.
But, when he came again, it was as though
The night had fallen at noontide; all was changed.

    Guin. What time was that?

    Elaine.   Ah, madam, thou canst date
My sorrow with thy joy.

    Guin. [*Rising suddenly.*] What dost thou say?

    Elaine. Nay, be not angered: so it chanced to fall,
In that same hour when thou, new crowned a Queen,
Didst come from Cameliard as Arthur's bride—
My love was lost. 'Twas Lancelot brought thee here.

    Guin. Ay, was it so? In truth I had forgot.
Yes, sure, 'twas he. And now thou think'st that I
Can win thy love again! How shall that be?

    Elaine. Hold Lancelot to thy side, I ask but that!
Let him not go to-day upon this quest,
Whence none, perchance, shall live to win his way
Back to King Arthur's court. Ah, bind him here,
That so my love, by some sweet chance, may find
The path it missed before, and creep again
Back to that heart that once did seem its home!
Thou dost not answer?

    Guin.   Hush, what sound is that?

Chaunt of the Knights without.

Look not to thy sword,
   Fame is but a breath,
That, for all reward,
   Brings thee only death.
Rise, and go forth with us who seek the Grail,
   Winning for reward
   Fame that shall not fail.

Elaine. [*Who has gone to the back.*] It is the chaunt
   of those who seek the Grail.
See, they make ready.   Lancelot is not there!
   Guin. Go, leave me now, for I must speak with him,
And think what I may do to serve thee best.
   Elaine. [*Kissing her hand.*] Ah, would I owned thy
   crown that may command,
Or thou my love, that so he needs must yield!
                       [*Exit* ELAINE.
   Guin. And would I ne'er had seen thee, for thy words
Have set my heart on fire!   Can it be so?
That then when first we met his love did change?
It is not so, and his own lips shall speak
And say 'tis false, or else I shall go mad.

Enter LANCELOT.

Ah, thou art here.   Why is thy mind so bent
To leave the court?   The King would know the cause.
Think'st thou, because thy favour stands so high
In fame of earthly deeds, that thou shalt win
This heavenly crown?
   Lan.   Indeed, I think not so.
His eyes alone shall see that holy cup,
Whose soul stands clear of sin.
   Guin.   What boots it then
To adventure all upon a hopeless quest?

Lan. Ay, hopeless, for I may not touch the goal.
Yet once, when I lay stricken nigh to death,
By this same vessel of the Sangrael
My hurt was cured ; now, when my heart is pierced,
Though by no mortal stroke of sword or spear,
Perchance again that same sweet miracle
May heal my deeper wound.

    Guin.   I know thy wound.

    Lan. If that were so I should be shamed indeed !

    Guin. Indeed, 'tis so. Elaine was here but now.
I did not dream that all the world could show
So fair a maid. No marvel that thy heart
Is sick with love.

    Lan.   Madam, I love her not !

    Guin. Nay, that is false : think it no shame to own
What, in some angry fit, thy tongue denied.

    Lan. My shame lies deeper, seeing I once vowed
A love that now lies dead.

    Guin.   Elaine's soft eyes
Will find Love's tomb, and charm it back to life.
Go to her now, and plead thy suit again ;
I'll warrant you will find her not too hard,
Your wooing is half done.

    Lan.   Urge me no more,
For here, by Heaven, I swear I love her not.

    Guin. Then wherefore wouldst thou enter on this
         quest ?

    Lan. Nay, madam, in thy pity, spare me that !

    Guin. I will be answered. Am I not thy Queen ?

    Lan. Thou art indeed, and therefore hast thy will !
I had thought to pass away and leave behind
The dear remembrance of thy loyal love
I once deserved. But now that too has gone,
For thou wouldst wring the secret from my lips
That brands me traitor.

    Guin.   Traitor !

    Lan.   Ay ! 'Tis true,
And thou hast known it, else thy gracious heart
Were not so pitiless : 'twas for this I've seen

Those veiled eyes cloak the hate they scorned to tell,
When, by some evil chance, their gaze met mine ;
For this thy gentle smile took sudden flight
When I passed by.
  Guin.   No! no! no more, no more!
  Lan. Nay, madam, drink thy vengeance to the
   fill.
I leave the court because I love its Queen!
         [*Flings himself at her feet.*
  Guin. I did not hear thee ; speak that word again.
  Lan. Ay, once again, I love thee ; all my shame
Lies naked at thy feet ; I do but crave
That here my life may end.
  Guin.   Nay, do not rise.
There's something I would say, yet know not how;
For if thy life must end, then so must mine.
You cannot guess my shame.
  Lan.   Thou hast no shame,
Save that which my base love hath laid on thee !
  Guin. Indeed, I have. Oft when we kneel and
   pray
Before God's image bleeding on the Cross,
We cheat our souls, for our vain hearts still seek
The manhood, not the God : 'twas so with me.
That hour when Arthur came, it seemed as though
Christ's hand had beckoned, and I knelt to him,
And, in the mist of worship, thought I saw
The wingèd heart of love. But when you came,
His great ambassador from Camelot,
I saw Love's heart indeed, and knew I loved—
But not the King.
  Lan.   What say'st thou ? Not the King ?
Wouldst make me mad ?
  Guin.   Ah me, that home-coming
When we two rode in silence side by side,
And all my heart was hungry for a word !
The blossoms of the springtime turned to flame—
And yet you spoke not ; now it is too late.
         [*She moves away.*

Lan. [*Rising.*] No, not too late, unless those lips
are false.

Ah! hear me now—thou wouldst have heard me
then.

My lonely love I could have borne alone,
Counting this mortal life too short a term
Of exile for my sin ; but now that's past,
And, through the darkness, like a sudden star,
Thy heart stands clear, lighting our sweeter way.
Nay, do not turn thy face, thou knowest 'tis so.
Love speaks at last—and Love will be obeyed.

> [*He moves towards her, and she turns as if to
> yield to his embrace when the chant of
> the* Knights *breaks forth again, and the
> movement is arrested.*

> Look not to thy love,
> Love that lives an hour ;
> Heaven's voice above
> Calls thee from her bower.
> Rise, and go forth, with us who seek the Grail,
> Winning from above
> Love that shall not fail.

Guin. Yea, truth, 'tis love that speaks ! But not
our love,
The love of Heaven, of honour, and of—him.

> Rise and go forth, with us who seek the Grail,
> Winning from above
> Love that shall not fail.

It is their voice that calls, and thou wilt go.
I thought to hold thee here—I may not now.
Lan. My shame is dumb ; yet, in thy purer heart,
I may find grace to save what still remains
Of my wrecked soul : my trust stands all in thee.
Guin. Nay, trust thyself.
Lan.   Thy word must be my law.
Guin. Wait not for that : a woman is too weak
To guard what's best in what she loves the best.

We shall not speak again.   [*Exit* GUINEVERE.
    Lan.   Ay, once again,
When from thy lips shall come the dread command
That sends me hence ; and like a flaming sword
Love bars the gate of this new paradise
Which love hath won ; yet through the desert night
Of life's long pilgrimage, one star shall stay,
And when death comes at last, to end our quest,
My fainting heart shall quicken at the thought,
'Twas thou didst bid me go.

                    Enter a SQUIRE.

                        Ah, thou art here.
Put on my sword.
            [*The trumpet sounds as* ARTHUR *enters, pre-*
                ceded by a procession of Priests *and*
                Choristers *chaunting the song of the Grail,*
                while the hall fills with a throng of
                Knights. ARTHUR *and* GUINEVERE
                take their places on the throne, on the steps
                of which stands ELAINE *next the* QUEEN.

            The Chaunt of the Grail.

        Look not to thy sword,
          Fame is but a breath,
        That, for all reward,
          Brings thee only death.
    Rise, and go forth with us who seek the Grail,
          Winning for reward
        Fame that shall not fail.

        [*At the close of the chaunt* PERCIVAL *comes*
            forward from the group of the Knights
            of the Grail and kneels before ARTHUR.
    Per. Here, at thy feet, for all whose vows are sworn,
I kneel and crave thy favour ere we go.
What strange new ways our wandering feet will press,

What dread adventures wait us, none can tell.
Yet this we know, our fealty to thee
Shall stand unbroken, and through all the world
We bear the spotless blazon of thy fame!

Arth. Rise, Percival, and ye who kneel with him,
Take your new way; ye have our leave to go;
Which yet, if that might be, we could withhold.
The magic circle of our Table Round
Is broken here: wherefore, in truth, my heart
Is sore within me, and my lips hold back
The message of Farewell. Yet must it be;
For well I know your vows are sworn to Him
Whose voice outbids the mandate of a king.
Therefore ride forth—we wait your glad return!

> [PERCIVAL *passes out, followed by the other*
> Knights of the Grail, *who kneel as they*
> *pass the throne. At the last comes*
> LANCELOT. ARTHUR *stops him.*

Arth. Nay, Lancelot, what is this?
Lan.   My lord, I too
Would take those vows that bind me to this quest.
Arth. [*To* GUINEVERE.] Didst thou not speak with
      him?
Guin.   I did, my lord.
Arth. Then had thy voice no power?
Guin.   In truth, I think
Some mightier voice than mine doth bid him go.
Arth. Then I must speak: this quest is not for thee.
For thy rich manhood hath a holier task—
Here, by thy King, to fight for this poor world
Till that last call which sheathes our swords in sleep.
Lan. My lord, thou knowest me not. I am not fit
To stand by thee.
Arth.   Nay, Lancelot, it is thou
That dost not know thyself for what thou art!
This crippled realm, how shall it find the goal,
If thou, the strongest, who hast been our staff,
If thou, the mightiest, who hast been our shield,
And thou, the gentlest, that art now our guide,

Seek thine own way towards Heaven; and so dost
    steal
The sun's bright rays wherewith to seek the sun,
Leaving this lonely world to grope its way
In darkness to the end ?   Thou shalt not go!
    Lan. My lord, did I but know myself as strong
As is the weakest of these knights whose vows
Were sworn but now, it would not need thy voice
To bid me stay.
    Arth.   Still thy resolve stands firm ?
Then thou shalt hear a sager voice than ours.
Old Merlin, by whose mystic craft we read
The unturned page of Time, stand forth and speak!
                    [MERLIN *steps forward.*
    Mer.   All shall seek the Holy Grail,
           All and all save one shall fail.
    Arth. Nay, leave thy riddles ; shall he go or stay ?
    Mer.   Fate doth not answer yea or nay.
           Love shall bid him go or stay!
           Love the best, or love the worst,
           Holiest love, or love accurst.
    Arth. Say on. What is this love that bids him go ?
    Mer. I can but read the words that Fate hath writ.
    Arth. Then we have done with Fate. Go, get thee
    hence,
And never more shall that dark face of thine
Pass, like a withered shadow, through these halls!
    Mer.   I go hence, yet Fate shall stay,
           Till the dawn of that dread day ;
           He Pendragon's son shall slay
           That is born with the May !
        [*As* MERLIN *goes out the hall grows darker,
           and the sunset at the back gleams more
           brightly.*
    Guin. My lord, I pray you call him back again !
    Arth. Nay, heed him not, my Queen—nor, Lancelot,
    thou !
For if indeed Love speaks with double voice,
One base, one noble, then be sure my lips

Do bear the nobler message ; for the world
Tells of no higher, purer love than that
Of brother unto brother : such in truth
Is my great love for thee, that bids thee stay !
    Lan. I know not how to answer for myself !
Yet, once before, when we were at debate
The verdict of our Queen did end all strife.
I crave it now, her word shall be my law !
    Arth. Then thou shalt stay : for she and I are one,
With but one voice, one tongue, one heart, one soul !
Now, Guinevere, declare thy will.
    Guin.   My lord,
A woman is too weak to rule men's hearts.
    Arth. Not so, my Queen. Hath not thy purer heart,
Sole ruler over him who rules this realm,
Won, from rude wars, that sweeter crown of peace
That smiles upon our land from sea to sea ?
And wouldst thou fail me now ? when on thy word
The welfare of a kingdom waits in doubt—
Wouldst thou be dumb ?
    Guin.   Indeed, indeed I would.
    Arth. Nay, I command thee—speak as I would
         speak !
    Elaine. Ay, madam, speak ! My life lies in thy word.
    Guin. [*After a pause, and without looking at*
         LANCELOT.] My lord, I do thy bidding—
         Lancelot, stay!
         [*The* Knights of the Grail *file past, singing as*
           they go.

        Ere those lips be dumb
           That would bid thee stay ;
        Ere the night be come,
           Rise, and come away!
     We, who go forth to seek the Holy Grail,
           Win, ere night be come,
           Light that shall not fail.

ACT II.

The Queen's Maying.

SCENE :—*The slope of a hill in spring-time studded with bushes of whitethorn. A company of* Maidens, *garlanded with white may, descend the slope. They are followed by* GUINEVERE *and her* Ladies.

The May Song.

RE upon its snowy bed
    Lies the firstborn of the spring,
Ere the crocus lifts its head,
    Or the swallow finds its wing,
       Love is here :
Say ye then Earth's flowers shall fade ?
    We shall tell ye nay :
Love, the first of all flowers made,
    Lives from May to May.

He beneath whose sun-kissed feet
    Daisies rise to kiss the sun,
Lily, rose, and meadow-sweet,—
    Love, that is all flowers in one,
       Love is here.
Heed not then the blooms that fall,
    Dying with the day,
Love, the sweetest flower of all,
    Lives from May to May.

Guin. Here, on the verge of this untravelled wood,
Beneath Love's flowering banner, we have set

Our camp of war. For, know ye, ladies all,
That dread adventure whereunto ye are called
Is no poor mockery of a tournament
Such as our lords love, jousting for a prize !
Our cause is mortal ; and those unseen swords
We women wield are forged to pierce men's hearts.
Whereat, if any cheek grow white with fear,
Let its poor owner straightway quit the field.
Nay, all are brave ? 'tis well. Ere day had dawned
Our scouts and spies, which are the wingèd birds,
Reported that a band of swaggering knights
Did challenge our approach ; 'gainst them we war.
Yet hear me—not like timorous men who find
Their courage grow from fellowship in fear,
Wherefore in serried ranks they face their foe.
Our greater strength hath ever best been proved
In single combat : so we fight to-day ;
Nor need these fairer faces be encased
In casques of steel ; that never was our plan—
For so indeed we should but hide from view
All Love's bright armoury that lodges there.
But, truth, I waste my breath where all are skilled
In these same arts of war. Therefore set forth,
Each on her chosen way, for in this wood
Lurks many a pleasant bower o'er-roofed with green,
Where moss and harebells weave a patterned floor
With shifting tracery of added gold,
Shot from the sun's eyes, peeping through the
    boughs
Of flowering thorn. There should each lady lead
Her conquered knight, that so, by gentler arts,
Her love may cure the wounds that Love hath
    made.
So, fare we all till sunset. Haste, away !

> [*As they move towards the wood* DAGONET
> *rushes in and falls on his knees before
> the* QUEEN. *He bears a large rough
> garland of flowers hanging about his
> neck like a horse-collar.*

Dag. [*Who is trembling with mock fear.*] Sweet
ladies, save me though ye love me not!
I am sore pressed.

Guin.   What, hath some beast pursued thee?

Dag. Ay, truth, a most sweet beast, yet fearsome,
too.

Clarissant. I pray you, madam, let us call these
knights.
We are in danger else.

Guin.   Is this your valour,
That so you quake at shadows? Shame on ye!

Dag. Ay, shame, for here is a beast that will harm
no lady, though at this budding season 'tis very fatal
to man.

Guin. I would hear more of this beast. What
form hath it?

Dag. Well, to be plain yet modest withal, and not
too curious, it is in all things shaped like a woman.

Guin. Truly, a very monstrous woman that would
so pursue a fool.

Dag. Faith, there be many such, though 'tis only
your sage fool that fears them.

Guin. Rise, Dagonet, and tell us how it chanced.

Dag. Then stiffen your sinews, for 'tis a heart-
shaking legend. Hither came I through the wood,
thinking of naught, and so counting myself wise
beyond my years, when of a sudden I espied a maid
who tended a herd of swine; whereat, I do confess
it, I fell a-weeping bitterly, for surely never was
mortal woman so fitly employed.

Clarissant. You hear him, madam.

Guin. Nay, let him run on.

Dag. Ay, 'tis the finish that will cause ye to
quake. For this same maid, not content with her
most righteous calling, and haply moved by my tears,
most artfully flung this halter about my neck, and
swore a most villainous oath that she loved me well.
Whereat I, being, as 'tis known, only half a fool,
slipped from her embrace, and fled incontinently.

Guin. Now thou art half a man, and therefore a most complete fool, that could so dread to be loved.

Dag. Wherein thou art wrong, for I have a leaning that way, being very tenderly fashioned, and with a taste for red lips. But alack, I am troubled with a most constant heart that goes not with love!

Guin. How say you? Is it so wise to rail against constancy?

Dag. Nay, I would question thee. Canst tell me now what is most like to a river that drains to the sea?

Guin. Faith, I cannot.

Dag. Why, a maiden who weeps in the rain.

Guin. Where hast thou seen that?

Dag. Last night, where I sheltered from the storm, there passed a lady sobbing as she rode, and with her tears the rain kept even tune; 'twas a sweet contest, yet I'll warrant her eyes outstayed the drippings of the sky.

Guin. Knew you her face?

Dag. 'Twas laid so low upon her palfrey's neck I saw it not.

Guin. Go, fool, on your way.

Dag. Ay, madam, by your leave, for I must seek the King, who comes from hunting. In May-time your King and your fool were ever very prettily assorted.

[*He goes up the hill singing.*

The cuckoo's note doth haunt the May,
And some are glad,
And some grow mad,
But the fool goes singing on his way.

[*Exit* DAGONET. *As he goes the* QUEEN *stands wrapt in thought.*

Clarissant. Nay, madam, see, 'tis noon; we waste our day.

Guin. [*Rousing herself.*] Truly; lift up your voices: let us on.

May Song.

Dreaming 'neath a whitened thorn,
  Like a rose-leaf on the snow,
Lovers! ere the day be worn,
  Ye shall find him and shall know,
    Love is here.
And, at nightfall when ye part,
  Whispering shall say :
Love is lord of every heart,
  Love is lord of May.

> [*The* Ladies *wander off through the wood
> preceded by the company of singing
> maidens, whose voices grow gradually
> fainter as they are lost in the distance,
> and at the last* GUINEVERE *follows
> slowly, and as she goes off,* MORGAN
> *enters, and stands gazing after her,
> while at the same time* MERLIN *appears
> on the rising path above.*

Morg. March on, my Queen, in all thy bravery!
He that is lord of May and of thy heart,
Blind leader of the blind, shall draw thee on,
Where Lancelot waits for thee, love's slave and ours.
  Mer. The scabbard's gone, but England's lord
    Holds till death the naked sword.
  Morg. [*Seeing him.*] What wouldst thou now whose
    work is wellnigh done?
May-day is here, and we, thy ministers,
Need no fresh spur to hasten Fate's decree.
  Mer. [*Approaching her.*] At dawn I heard the
    splashing of the mere,
And saw that jewelled scabbard sink and sink
Till, like a glittering rainbow, down the deep
It vanished, and the shuddering tide grew still.
Dost thou know aught of this?
  Morg.   Not I, forsooth!
  Mer. Thou liest, for I tracked thee in thy theft,

And saw thee creep beside the sleeping King,
Whose hand held fast that naked blade which
    gleamed,
A bar of quivering moonlight, by his side.
Thou hast stol'n the scabbard, but no mortal hand
Shall take the sword.

    Morg.   What then ? thyself didst say—
The scabbard's worth doth far outweigh the sword.

    Mer. To him, but not to thee. 'Tis naught to thee :
Who steals the scabbard doth but draw the sword ;
Who holds the sword, holds all save life, and wins,
Though life be spent, a deathless crown from death.

    Morg. Whose hand shall take it then, when death
        draws near ?

    Mer.   When those Queens of Night shall steer
        Arthur's barge across the mere,
        She who long ago did bring
        England's sword to England's King,
            She shall claim Excalibur !
                    [*Exit* MERLIN.

    Morg. Croak on, let Death but come ; we'll chance
        the rest !

              Enter MORDRED.

    Mord. Whose voice was that ?

    Morg.   'Twas Merlin's, who grows old,
And babbles like a child. What is thy news ?

    Mord. Beyond our hope ; Ryons and Mark are
        joined
In equal strength of war, and, by this hour,
Their glittering squadrons, like a serpent, coil
Around Caerleon's walls.

    Morg.   Whence got you this ?

    Mord. Sir Morys from Caerleon rode post haste
To warn our Master. He will ride no more.
                    [*Touching his sword.*

    Morg. 'Tis well ; your men keep watch on every road ?

Mord. Ay, all are guarded : let but this day pass
With no unwelcome note to wake the King,
Then war may shriek its loudest ; all is sure.
   Morg. Hast thou forgotten Lancelot ?
   Mord. [*In alarm.*]   What of him ?
   Morg. Nay, track him through the wood, and thou
      shalt learn.
Come hither ; see where, trembling, hand to hand, ‗
With speechless answering eyes, they woo the spring.
Love sets the snare, but the caged bird is ours.
For ere night's dusky arms enfold the sun,
Lancelot shall be thy partner and thy slave.

            [*Exeunt* MORGAN *and* MORDRED. *The May
                 Song is heard faintly in the distance.*

            Enter SIR LAVAINE *and* CLARISSANT.

   Lavaine. Dost think our love will live from May to
      May ?
   Clarissant. Nay, ask me that when May-day comes
      again.
   Lavaine. Ah, tell me now !
   Clarissant.   I'll tell thee all I know.
If thou dost woo me well, I'll love thee well,—
Should no one woo me better !
   Lavaine.   Wouldst thou be wooed
That art already won ?
   Clarissant.   Most surely, sir !
Who holds my heart must win it every day ;
And when 'tis won, 'tis then it must be wooed
And won again.
   Lavaine.   Why, 'twas but yesterday
That thou didst swear thy love would last till death.
   Clarissant. Ay, that was yesterday.
   Lavaine.   And shall thine oath
Live but an hour ?
   Clarissant.   What is there in these oaths
That you poor men so fondly cherish them ?
Perchance they fit your duller brains, which seek,

With empty words, to bind the unborn hours.
But we do wrong to humour you in this.
We should not swear at all, knowing full well
There's no to-morrow in a woman's heart,
Which hath its yesterday of joy or pain,
Whose savour, lingering on our lips to-day,
Makes all the present half a memory—
The future all a blank.   Then ask me not
If I shall love thee when the year is worn ;
I loved thee yesterday : so be content.

   Lavaine. Ah, but thou lovest to-day ?

   Clarissant.   To-day is young ;
Ask me at sundown, I will tell thee then.
             [*Exit laughing, and he following her.*

     Enter GUINEVERE *and* LANCELOT.

   Guin. The wood is dark.   Let us be in the sun.

   Lan. 'Twas dark ere yet the glory of thy face
Came, like a golden message from the sun.
And now, beneath this open vault of day,
'Twould change again to night wert thou not here.

   Guin. I had a foolish fear I should not find thee.

   Lan. Nay, Guinevere, thou know'st that could not
    be.

   Guin. Indeed, 'tis true, for wandering alone
Across the leafy screen that hedged my way,
From every side I heard the echoing laugh
Of Love's encounter.   Then the wood grew still,
And, softer than the silence, came the sound
Of whispered vows from lips but newly met ;
And then, beneath an opening arch of green,
Two lovers passed, with hand in hand locked
    close.
Ah, Lancelot ! I was lonely as a child
Locked in a darkened room.   I called thee then ;
Didst thou not hear me ?

   Lan.   Ay, and saw thee, too.

   Guin. Thou didst not answer ?

Lan.   Nay, forgive me, sweet!
I could but watch thee.
    Guin.   That was cruel, sir.
    Lan. 'Twas but an instant.
    Guin.   No, it was a year!
And in that year a thousand thronging fears
With devil faces perched amid the boughs.
    Lan. What were thy fears?
    Guin.   So many all in one:
That I should lose thee.
           [LANCELOT *putting his arms round her.*
    Lan.   Never, until death.
    Guin. Ah, speak not so of death! I have seen a
       face
That frighted me like death.
    Lan. [*Starting.*]   Whose face and where?
    Guin. Within the wood. 'Twas Merlin's, but so
       old,
Lancelot, so old and worn I knew it not.
    Lan. Those empty words of his do haunt thee
       still.
I wonder at thy fears.
    Guin.   Nay, scold me not.
There's nothing haunts me when I have thee near.
Love shuts the door on all things save itself,
On all that's past, on all that is to come
When thou art by! Tell me, 'tis so with thee?
    Lan. Ay, sweet, 'tis so.
    Guin.   Ah, say it once again!
I could not live, Lancelot, if in thy heart
There lurked the tiniest little ache or pain
Love might not cure.
    Lan.   Thou knowest all my heart;
And in my love, which knows no law but love,
The future and the past are drowning straws
Caught in the full tide of our present joy,
That neither ebbs nor flows.

[*He holds her in a close embrace as* MORGAN
and MORDRED *enter stealthily ; at the
same time is heard the sound of distant
thunder, and the scene darkens.*

Morg. Dost mark them well ?

Lan. Ambition, honour, duty, all that life
Once held most dear, by thy sweet will subdued,
Now wear Love's livery and would serve Love's
Queen.

[*The thunder is heard again and nearer.*

Guin. [*Starting.*] What sound was that ? See, it
grows dark again !

Lan. 'Tis but a cloud.

Guin. It came like sudden night.
Let us go in. [*Thunder again.*
Ah, 'tis the thunder's bolt
That cracks the sky !

Lan. Nay, tremble not ; 'twill pass,
And leave Heaven's deeper blue. What shouldst
thou fear ?

Guin. I know not. Hold me closer, closer still,
That so my heart may catch the fearless tune
Of thy heart's steadfast music. Now I am brave,
And could be always, wert thou always here.
So let us on. Yet tell me o'er again—
Ah, I do tease thee ; 'tis but this once more—
Tell me, whate'er befall, that thou art mine !

Lan. For ever and for ever I am thine.

[*A crash of thunder and a lightning flash.*

Mord. [*Looking after them.*] He lies, my Queen ;
not thine, but mine till death !

ACT III.

The Black Barge.

Scene :—*A vaulted chamber opening on to the river.*

As the curtain draws up enter Sir Lancelot, *followed by* Sir Kay, Sir Gawaine, *and* Sir Agravaine.

Lancelot.

IR MORYS slain?

Gaw.   Ay, murdered.

Lan.   But by whom?

Kay. That's still to find. Know you from whence he came?

Lan. Straight from Caerleon, whither, as I heard,
He rode with sealed advices for the King.

Kay. Said I not well? Arthur hath been forestalled.

Lan. Why, 'twas but yesterday the King did note
His long delay.

Gaw.   It was but yesternight
We found him murdered.

Lan.   Sirs, if this be so,
There's something more than murder.

Kay.   More, in truth!
Lancelot, some traitor lurking near the throne,
In secret league with Arthur's enemies,
By this same villainous act now stands possessed
Of what the King should know.

Agra.   What must be done?

Gaw. Let Lancelot speak.

Lan. I'll straightway to the King
And tell him all. Then, should we win his leave,
At nightfall we'll to horse, nor draw the rein
Until Caerleon's towers cut the sky.

       [*Exeunt* KAY, AGRAVAINE, *and* GAWAINE.

    During the next speech MORDRED *enters.*

Whose hand is here? Of all our knights but one
In my most secret heart dare stand accused
Of this foul deed.   [*Turns and sees* MORDRED.
       Mordred! Morys is slain!

  Mord. Sir Morys slain! Nay, 'tis some idle jest.

  Lan. That is not all; the advices that he bore—
Are stolen.

  Mord.   Stolen? Is it possible?

  Lan. Ay, sir, and true; which news must to the
    King.

  Mord. Most surely: yet not now; he is fatigued,
And would not be disturbed. To-morrow, sir.

  Lan. Nay, sir, to-day; an hour's delay may risk
The safety of his throne, perchance his life.

  Mord. Well, sir, what then?

  Lan. [*In amazement.*]   What then?

  Mord.   Nay, spare thy skill;
'Tis aptly feigned; in faith, I'd say 'twas true
Did I not hold a key that locks thy heart.

  Lan. What dost thou mean?

  Mord.   I mean, should Arthur pass
He leaves behind a kingdom, and a Queen
Who loves him not.

  Lan.   Who says so foully lies!

  Mord. Lancelot, throw off this mask, it fits thee
    not;
Be what thou art, nor fear what thou wouldst be.
Let candour answer candour. It was I
Who slew this messenger. His papers here
Bring the rich news that ere a week be past
Caerleon's gates must yield to the assault

Of Ryons' siege, whose vengeance stays not there ;
The King himself is doomed ; and, the King dead,
His throne is mine, and thine his widowed Queen.

Lan. Traitor! I knew it.   Thou shalt to the King,
In whose dread presence, from that villain's throat,
I'll force those words again.

Mord.   I dare thy worst!
Yet breathe one word and I will tell a tale
Shall make thee cower like a beaten hound.

Lan. Thou'st naught to tell.

Mord.   What! are her kisses naught?
Fie, sir, for shame!   So then thou didst not guess
I lurked so near, and saw thee lip to lip,
Cuddling beneath the may ; that is love's trick,
Who blindfold deems that all the world is blind.
Now to the King!   See, sir, the way is clear.
What!   Wouldst thou pause?   Hast thou no heart to
      win
That sweet reward that waits thy loyal zeal——
A traitor's death?

Lan.   What were that death to me?

Mord. True! but the Queen?

Lan.   Vile wretch!
                    [*Movement towards* MORDRED.

Mord.   Look where she comes ;
Take thought with her, she will advise thee well.
We men are rash, a woman's subtler wit
Serves better in such case.   Truth, but she's fair—
So fair,—why, Lancelot, I repent me now
I kept not this sweet morsel for mine own.

Lan. Out of my sight!

Mord. [*Aside.*]   His tongue is safely gagged ;
Yet he's but half corrupt, I'll trust him not.   [*Exit.*

LANCELOT *stands in despair as* GUINEVERE *enters.*

Guin. Who went from thee?

Lan.   'Twas Mordred.

Guin. [*Approaching him.*]   Lancelot,

Some evil hath befall'n!

Lan.   'Tis naught. [*He turns away.*

Guin.   'Tis much

Can make thee turn from me; ah, but I'll know it!
Didst thou not swear our love should cure all ill?
Then tell me all.

Lan.   Caerleon is besieged;

Should succour fail 'twill yield to Ryons' arms.

Guin. Who brings these tidings?

Lan.   Mordred.

Guin.   And the King?

Lan. Knows naught.

Guin. [*With sudden horror.*] Knows naught? Lan-
    celot, ah no! ah no!

Sure thou wouldst tell the King.

Lan.   Indeed I would.

Guin. Then wherefore pause?

Lan.   Oh, had I died but then,

In that sweet hour when first I learned thy love,
I had been happy!

Guin.   *What* is in thy heart?

Lan. Mordred is false.

Guin.   False?

Lan.   Ay, 'tis he that's hatched

This plot against the King, whereby he thinks
To seize the throne.

Guin.   Then thou shalt prove him false

And save the King.

Lan.   I dare not.

Guin.   Dare not?

Lan.   No:

All, all is known.

Guin.   To whom?

Lan.   To him; he was there

Beside us in the May; his trait'rous hand
Grips at my throat and makes me traitor too.

Guin. No, no, that cannot be. Ah, look not so!
What wouldst thou do?

Lan.   Nay, ask what have I done?

Was there no lamp in Heaven to stay our feet?
Was the night starless, that we needs must wait
Till love's torch, setting all the world ablaze,
Lights up love's ruinous way? Ah, Guinevere,
I'd die a hundred deaths but now to win
One hour of life that's past; ay, one short hour,
So I might drag this devil to the throne
And shout his villainies in every ear.

Guin. Then do it now.

Lan.   I cannot.

Guin.   Yea, thou canst!
Who is there that should stay thee, 'tis not I!
Let love go down the wind, what boots it now?
Look to thyself; think not of all that's lost.
That is all mine: for thee there still remains
Thy soldier's honour, take it, keep it pure.

Lan. What have I said?

Guin.   Ah, go! [*Throws herself on couch.*

Lan. [*Throwing himself at her feet.*] My Queen!
      My Queen!
There's nothing in the world to win or lose
Can count beside thy love. I lied but now;
King, honour, country, all that knighthood boasts
Of faith and loyalty in life or death
Weighs not against the memory of one kiss
From thy dear lips.

Guin.   Then thou art mine again.
To hear thee say that all the world was naught
Against our love hath made me mad for joy.
Yet stay not now; I have a thought to think,
And needs must be alone.

Lan.   Yet, ere I go,
Hear this one word: all that is left of life
Is thine to keep or thine to fling away,
So I may have thy love.

                              [*Exit* LANCELOT.

Guin.   Thou hast, indeed!
So all is won again, and all is lost!
So do we strive that we may have the more

To cast away : and now, when at my feet
He lays his sword, his life, ay, and his soul,
I do but long to find some better way
To give him all again ; ay, all again!   [*Looks off.*
It is the King.   How may I find that way ?

Enter ARTHUR.

   Arth.   Ah, thou art here.   I bring thee such sad
  news
As needs must wring thy heart.
   Guin.   What news, my lord ?
   Arth. Elaine is dead!
   Guin.   Dead !   Who hath told thee this ?
   Arth. There, yonder by the shore, her body lies
Who, while she lived, was named the Fair Elaine.
Canst thou not weep ?
   Guin.   Truly, my lord, I think
I've lost the use of tears.
   Arth.   Thou wouldst have wept
Hadst thou been there when down the vacant
    stream
That black barge floated, like a speck of night,
Blown on the winds of dawn ; and on its deck,
Fallen as a feather from a white dove's wing,
Lay this new prize of Death ; whose cunning hands
Had wrought in such fair mimicry of life
That on her parted lips there lingered yet
The memory of a smile.
   Guin.   Why then, perchance,
She's happier far than some who needs must live
And smile no more.
   Arth.   It may be ; for that brow
Had caught from Death some secret of content
It knew not here, and, looking in those eyes,
Whose tears had ceased their traffic, I dared think,
If aught of sin was there, 'tis pardoned now.
   Guin. Of sin ?   What sin ?
   Arth.   Ay, for it must be so :

Some sin there was though unrecorded here ;
Some stain that smirched her seeming purity,
Which Lancelot, all too noble, could not urge ;
Else were it not in nature to refuse
So sweet a gift.
 Guin.   If that indeed be true,
Were it enough to shut the doors of love ?
 Arth. Enough ? What wouldst thou ask ?
 Guin.   Ay ! Ay ! enough,
Enough and more ! Yet, in some greater heart,
As his, or thine, methought that love might find
Forgiveness e'en for that.
 Arth.   Nay, wrong him not,
Whose upward gaze, set level with the stars,
Would lift from earth the soul he crowns with love,
Making her more than woman ; whence if she fall—
Like some lost planet hurled from highest Heaven—
She falls to endless night.
   [*During* ARTHUR'S *speech the distant throb of*
    a mournful march is heard slowly
    approaching.
 Guin.   Most like 'tis so,
And death the only way. What sound is that ?
 Arth. Up from the stream they bear her body
   hither,
Where it shall rest beneath this royal roof,
Till, with such liberal honours as befit
So fair a flower, 'tis set again in earth.
   [*The procession enters, headed by* MORDRED
    and MORGAN. *Four* Knights *bear*
    ELAINE *and are followed by a company*
    of Maidens.
 Morg. [*Aside to* MORDRED.] Her cheek grows pale ;
   she will betray herself.
   [*She passes across the stage and takes her place*
    behind the QUEEN. *At a sign from*
    MORDRED *the* Knights *move forward*
    till they come to where GUINEVERE *is*
    standing rigid and motionless. Then

they stop in silence till GUINEVERE,
without turning, cries in agony.

Guin. Go on! and set it down!

Mord. [*Coming forward.*] Madam, by your
leave,
In that white hand of death a letter lies,
Whose seal we dared not break, for 'tis inscribed
"To Guinevere, the Queen."

Arth. [*To* GUINEVERE.] Then break the seal,
Which hides perchance some secret of her love
We know not yet.

> [GUINEVERE *tries to approach the bier, but
> cannot touch the body; then with a
> despairing appeal she turns to* ARTHUR.

Guin. I cannot! Give it me.

> [ARTHUR *takes the letter which* GUINEVERE
> *opens and lets fall, staggering back into
> the arms of* MORGAN, *whose eyes gleam
> in triumph.*

Morg. Nay, madam, nay; what is it moves thee
thus?

> [MORDRED *picks up the letter and gives it to
> the* KING.

Arth. [*Reading.*] " I that was named Elaine of
Astolat,
Whose mortal love for Lancelot passed all measure,
Seeing he loves another, choose to die."
We knew not this. Go, call Sir Lancelot here.

Guin. My lord, my lord——

> [*She struggles forward as though to stop the*
> KING'S *command, and then swoons into*
> MORGAN'S *arms.*

Arth. Look to the Queen.

> [MORGAN *and her* Women *support her from
> the stage, and at the same time the* Knights
> *lay the body of* ELAINE *under the alcove,
> and then exeunt, leaving* ARTHUR *and*
> MORDRED *alone.*

Mord. [*Aside.*] Ere Lancelot's blow can fall

I'll strike him to the heart.

Arth. [*Holding the letter.*]   If this be true,
'Tis strange that none had known.

Mord.   What's that, my lord?

Arth. What's here set down of Lancelot's later love.

Mord. Now would to Heaven those words had
      ne'er been writ
Or ne'er been read.

Arth.   Why so?

Mord.   Didst thou not note
How the Queen's soul was stirred?

Arth.   She is not used
To look on death; which, coming in such guise,
Might move our soldier hearts.

Mord.   Ay, but methought
It was Death's message and not Death itself
That turned those red lips white.

Arth.   Mordred, what's this?
Think you the Queen hath known of this same love?

Mord. Nay, I'll not answer that.

Arth.   Nay, but thou shalt.
What is to fear?

Mord.   My lord, thou art my King;
My sword is thine, and with that sword my life;
But with that life my loyal service ends,
And what is left thou wilt not ask of me.

Arth. Who is it that he loves?

Mord.   In sooth, I thought
What all the world had known was known to thee;
Were it not so these lips had still been dumb.
But now 'tis best 'twere said—he loves the Queen!
                         [*A pause.*

Arth. Who forged this lie? Nay, Mordred, 'tis not
      thou;
And yet I wonder, too, to find thee duped
By this poor tale bred in some baser soul
That loves not Lancelot.

Mord.   What! thou think'st 'tis false?
Why then, my lord, 'tis false.   I'll think so, too,

We'll speak of it no more.
 Arth.   Ay, but we will,
And track this running poison to its source,
Which else should turn all the pure springs of life
To pools of festering filth.

     Enter MORGAN *hurriedly.*

 Morg.   My lord, the Queen——
Why thou art pale! Nay, do not take it so;
'Twas but a sudden fit, and soon will pass.
  Arth. Morgan, come hither: know'st thou aught of
   this?
  Morg. Of what, my lord?
  Arth.   Of Lancelot's love for her——
The Queen?
  Morg. The Queen? Now who hath told thee this?
[*Turning to* MORDRED.] Shame on thee, shame! I
   pray you heed him not.
I would have cut my tongue out ere I'd spoken
Such evil of our mistress!
  Arth.   Let him be;
He doth but hint what every hawker cries.
  Morg. But he did wrong to speak, and thou to hear.
So sweet a lady, and at such an hour!
Were I a man, for all he is my child,
My sword should answer him.
  Mord. [*With assumed anger.*] Now this is more
Than I have will to bear! Why 'twas thyself
Didst tell how yesternight Sir Lancelot
Went to her bower alone.
  Arth.   Didst thou say so?
  Morg. In truth 'twas so; and hath been so
   before;
Yet did I think no wrong; and now I'm sure
He bore some message from the King himself.
  Arth. No, he did not.
  Morg.   Well, then be sure 'twas naught,
        E

And she shall prove it naught.
   Mord.   Nay, mother, nay,
Let us be honest!   Thou wouldst serve the Queen,
And so would I ; yet may we not be false
To him whom Heaven hath made her lord and
      ours.
How canst thou say 'twas naught?   Why, thou wast
      there
Beside me, when they kissed beneath the May.
   Arth. [*Turns slowly towards* MORGAN.] Tell him
      he lies.
   Morg.   My lord, my lord, I cannot. [*A pause.*
   Arth. There'll come a time when I shall know full
      well
This is a dream ; but now I'll play it out
As though 'twere true.   Go, get thee to the Queen.
   Morg. Think not too ill of her.
   Arth.   Nay, nor of thee. [*Exit* MORGAN.
[*To* MORDRED.] Go on, there's more to come Think
      you he knows
You lurked so near and saw him ?
   Mord.   Ay, most sure,
For now, with lying tongue, he goes about
Whispering that I have hatched some treacherous
      plot
Against thy throne and thee.
   Arth.   Why, then I think
This is some other Lancelot ye have met,
And this some other King !   He whom I knew
Was of all knights the bravest and the truest,
Serving a lord who could not have stood dumb
To hear his name befouled.

     LANCELOT *enters and approaches the* KING,
        who does not turn to him.

   Lan.   My lord, I am here.
Didst thou not send for me ?
   Arth.   Ay, so I did.

Lancelot, the scabbard of Excalibur
Is stol'n.

    Lan.   Who is the thief?

    Arth.   'Tis thou shalt say.

Dost think 'tis Mordred?

    Lan. [*Starting.*]   Why should I think so?

    Arth. Why not? I have heard there is some
    grosser charge

That thou wouldst bring against him.

    Mord. [*With assumed indignation.*] Nay, my good
    lord——

    Arth. Let Lancelot speak.

    Lan. [*After a pause.*] My lord, I bring no charge.

    Arth. Lancelot, think well; art sure thou know'st
    of naught

That should disturb our peace?

    Lan. [*After a pause.*]   Of naught, my lord.

    Arth. 'Tis well, 'tis well; then both of ye are true.

    Lan. Was it for this that thou didst send for
    me?

    Arth. Not so. Come hither, that thine eyes may
    feast

On this sweet picture.

        [LANCELOT *turns and starts at the sight of*
          ELAINE.

                 Nay, sir, note it well!

Death too hath gone a-maying, and hath plucked
Life's fairest flower—Elaine.

    Lan.   Methought she slept.

    Arth. Ay, past all waking; and wouldst know the
    cause?

    Lan. The cause?

    Arth.   Why she doth sleep; 'tis written here.

        [*He gives* LANCELOT *the letter; as the* KING
          watches him he reads it, and then falls
          on his knees before the bier.

Yet squander not thy grief; she heeds thee not.
The dead are dead; we give them ne'er a thought
Whose care is for the living; and, of all,

The most for thee. Wherever she may dwell,
This new-found beauty that hath lured thy heart,
We shall command her love. Nay, but we shall ;
For thou art known the courtliest, truest knight
That ever served a king. Then speak her name.

Lan. My lord, in truth——
Arth.   Nay, sir, who is this maid ?
Lan. There is no maid.
Arth.   Lancelot, thou sayest well ;
It is the Queen.
Lan.   Ah, no !
Arth.   Thou knowest 'tis so !
Thou art the thief who so hast stolen away
That scabbard that was worth a hundred swords.

Lan. Whose tongue hath told thee this ? here on
        my life
I'll answer him who dares accuse her honour.
Mord. Then answer me.
Lan.   Liar ! and so I will !
Yet first I'd have thee known for what thou art.
Traitor—I charge thee now.
Mord. [*With a sneer.*]   Said I not well ?

GUINEVERE *enters unseen.*

Arth. If *he* be traitor, what art thou whose sword
Strikes at my heart, yet would defend my throne ?
Prove this is false, and I'll believe him false ;
Prove that he lies, and I'll believe thee true.

Lan. Again I swear 'tis false.
Guin. [*Coming between them.*]   Nay, nay, 'tis true.
Lan. What hast thou done ?
Guin.   All that was left to do.
Arth. Ay, all ; there is no more to do or say ;
Death's banner floats above the blackened field,
The fight is ended and our day is done,
If this be so. But I'll not think 'tis so ;
Take back that word, and none shall know 'twas
        said !

Ah ! call it back again, and lift the pall
Death spreads upon my heart ; so shall I kneel
And bless thee, and this sword shall strike him
    dumb
That dares to whisper aught against my Queen.
                        [*She stands immovable.*
Is this so much to ask ? Ay, all too much !
There is no might can give back to the Spring
Its lowliest flower dead under changing skies ;
Then how should I, with winter at my heart,
Plead with the ruined summer for its rose ?
Thou hast no word ?
    Guin.   No word to cure what's done.
    Arth. [*To* LANCELOT.] Then arm thyself ; my
    sword shall find its sheath
Deep in thy heart.
    Lan.   Strike on ! Strike on ! I say,
For death is all I crave.
    Arth.   Then take it now.
        [ARTHUR *runs on* LANCELOT, *but the uplifted*
            sword drops from his hand.
I cannot kill thee ;
Some sudden palsy doth beat down this arm :
Its strength is gone. Yet think not 'tis the love
I bore thee once ; that's clean forgotten now.
Nor is it mercy ; for, had this same wrong
Chanced to the meanest hind that calls me King,
My sword had leapt in vengeance, and my soul
Had straight approved the deed. Yet here I stand
That cannot strike a blow in mine own cause.
Is this a curse that Heaven hath set on kings,
Who may not love nor hate like common men ?
Or is there some rank poison in a crown
That stamps the brand of coward on the brows
Of him who wears it ? Go, then, get thee hence !
Join with some foe that dares assault our throne ;
With Ryons, or with Mark, who hunger still
For open war. Ay, league thyself with them ;
And, in that hour, the hand that falters now,

In England's cause shall find its force again,
And strike thee to the earth.　Till then live on.

> [LANCELOT *goes out as* ARTHUR *turns to* MORDRED.

Leave us alone.　There's something left to say,
Mordred, that's not for thee.　　　　[*Exit* MORDRED.

Guin.　　　　　　　　　　And must I live?

Arth. It is too late to die.

Guin.　　　　　　　　　　Too late! too late!

Arth. Ay; would Death's marble finger had been
　　laid
On those sweet lips when first they linked with mine!

> [*Pointing to* ELAINE.

For, locked in Death's white arms, Love lies secure,
In changeless sleep that knows no dream of change.
'Tis Life, not Death, that is Love's sepulchre;
Where each day tells of passionate hearts grown
　　strange,
And perjured vows chime with the answering bell
That tolls Love's funeral.　If thou wouldst boast
Of this new sway a woman's wile hath won,
Go, tell the world thy heart hath slain a heart
That once had been a king's.　Yet that's not all,
Thou too hast been a Queen whose soul shone
　　clear,
A star for all men's worship, and a lamp
Set high in Heaven, whereby all frailer hearts
Should steer their course towards God; then, 'tis
　　not I
Whose life lies broken here, for at thy fall
A shattered kingdom bleeds.

> [*At the end of this speech a sound of warlike music is heard, and the stage fills with* Knights *headed by* GAWAINE *and* AGRAVAINE.

Gaw.　　　　　　　　　My lord! my lord!
Caerleon is besieged.

Enter MORDRED.

Kay.　　　　　　　And we thy knights,
Here armed and ready, do but wait to know
Our King's command.
　　Mord.　　　　　　Then let me lead them forth.
The chance is desperate, and thy greater life
Is England's, not thine own !
　　Arth.　　　　　　Nay, thou shalt stay ;
Thou art the one thing left my soul dare trust.
For, in this wreck of love, truth stands for all.
Sound out for war. [*Pointing to* GUINEVERE.] Yet,
　　　　pray you, use her well ;
We do not roughly trample down the flower
That grows upon a grave.　Then use her well,
For there entombed lies one who was my Queen.
Gawaine, I come.　Thy King shall lead thee forth ;
My sword is drawn, I want no scabbard now.
　　　　　　[ARTHUR *holds up his naked sword, and all*
　　　　　　　the Knights *raise their swords in answer*
　　　　　　　as the curtain falls.

ACT IV.

The Passing of Arthur.

Scene 1. *The* Queen's *prison in the Castle at Camelot.*
Door leading to the Queen's *chamber.* *Another*
door heavily barred. *Window at back.*

Gaoler *discovered keeping guard.* *As the scene opens*
knocking at outer door.

Gaoler.

HO knocks without ?
Mes. [*Without.*] One who bears a mes-
sage for the Queen.
[Gaoler *opens door and admits*
the Messenger.

Gaoler. What saith Sir Mordred ? May she see her
fool ?

Mes. Ay, I have brought him hither.

Gaoler. That will content her much ; she hath cried
often for her fool.

Mes. Yet methinks she shall suck but poor enter-
tainment from the fellow now : his wits are clean gone.
And, faith, he is not like to smile again.

Gaoler. What mean you, sir ?

Mes. The news of Arthur's death is now made
sure ; and what is worse, 'tis said 'twas Lancelot's
sword that struck him down.

Gaoler. Who shall tell this to the Queen ?

Mes. Within the hour Sir Mordred comes himself
To bear the news. Think you 'twill stir her heart ?

Gaoler. Indeed I think not so, look where she
comes,

Her white face like the head-stone at a grave,
O'er-lettered with the story of a day
That ended long ago.

Enter GUINEVERE. *She holds a bird in her hands.*

Guin. See what I've trapped : it fluttered at the
    bars
And fell there at my feet. I'd have it caged,
That I, its gaoler, may have leave to dream
That I am free ; and then, perchance, one day
This little bird will come and pray to me,
Who, being a Queen, must needs be merciful
And break its wicker walls.
    Gaoler. [*Taking the bird.*] I'll cage it now.
        [*He goes towards door, and she sees the*
        Messenger.
    Guin. Ah, sir, you're from the Court. Where is my
        fool,
Sir Dagonet ? Is that denied me too ?
'Twas not so much to ask.
    Mes.   Madam, he's here,
And yet so changed I fear he will not know thee.

Opens door, and DAGONET *enters.*

    Guin. That counts for naught. I scarce do know
        myself.
Come hither, Dagonet. Sirs, by your leave.
        [Gaoler *and* Messenger *exeunt.*
    Guin. Dost thou not know thy Queen ?
    Dag. Ay, very well, there were two of them : for
there was one, look you, that came with the Spring
from Cameliard, and she had a face that touched
Heaven ; and there was one that kept a poison on
her lip for Lancelot's kissing. And hark'e, last night
beneath the moon I saw them both kneeling beside a
grave.

Guin. Whose grave ?

Dag.   I know not, for the stone was bare,
And they did naught but weep.

Guin.   I'll tell thee, then :
This grave I think was Guinevere's who died
That hour when she was born; and these two
        Queens
Who through the night keep watch beside her tomb,
Are but her shadows fashioned for the masque
Which men call life ; poor puppets that must dance
While unseen fingers touch the trembling strings ;
But whence that music comes, from Heaven or
        Hell,
There's none shall say, till all life's lamps burn out
And Death stands forth to claim the harper's fee.

Enter Gaoler.

Gaoler. Make room, Sir Mordred comes.

Enter MORDRED.

                    [*Exeunt* Gaoler *and* DAGONET.
Mord. Great Queen, I bear thee news that sets thee
        free.

Guin. What news is that?

Mord.   Thy lord, the King, is dead.

Guin. Dead ! art thou sure? Why then, sir, *he* is
        free,
And I that was his gaoler may not weep ;
Yet count not that against me, for I think
Tears are not all.

Mord.   Truth, thou wert wrong to weep.
Dost thou not know 'twas Arthur's cruel will
That set thee in this prison ?

Guin.   Ay, I know,
That thou hast said 'twas so.

Mord.   And so it is :
But now I've come to break these prison bars,

And so give back unto our desert world
Life's sweetest rose that hungers for the sun.
   Guin. And who art thou whose new-found sovereignty
Rides o'er the King's decree ?
   Mord.   I am thy King.
   Guin. There is no King save one, and he is dead.
Yet if it was his will to leave me here,
Why, here I'll stay.
   Mord.   Nay, then thou dost not guess
The gift I bear thee ! Guinevere, those lips,
Moulded by Love's own hand, are not yet doomed
For Death's embrace : their kiss is for a king ;
Yet not like that dead lord whose bloodless soul
Wings to a frozen heaven : who wooes thee now
Is man, not god, and in his brimming veins
Run longings like thine own.
   Guin.   I thought till now
That I had suffered all ; but here I see
My shame doth but begin. 'Twas not enough
That through my sin, for all succeeding time,
Hell's mocking laugh shall haunt the voice of spring,
And plant its poisoned echo in each bower,
Where lovers' vows are sworn ! Nay, this is more ;
That she, whom love doth once make false to love,
Must henceforth bear the common brand of lust,
Seeming the painted toy that every man
May purchase at his price.
   Mord.   Why, thou dost dream !
Here at thy feet I lay an empire's throne,
Where thou in equal majesty shalt reign
Once more a Queen.
   Guin.   A wanton, not a Queen !
Who for this piece of gold thou call'st a crown
Would take thy murderer's kiss.
   Mord.   Nay, have a care !
My love lies near to hate.
   Guin.   I fear thy love ;
Thy hate is naught.
   Mord.   Truth, thou shalt find it more

Than thou hast ever dreamed.

> [*Shouts without, " Long live the King."*

Mord.   Dost hear that cry?
It is the echoing voice of England's knights,
Who hail me king.

> *Guin.*   And they were Arthur's knights?

> *Mord.* Ay, they loved Arthur well! Yet when
>   they learn—

As so they shall, for I will vouch it true—
'Twas Lancelot's sword did pierce him to the heart,
Their eyes will turn on her whose shameful sin
Made Lancelot false. See then, thy fate stands clear,
Thou art Death's bride, or mine—thy choice is free.

> *Guin.* Why then I choose to die. Yea, though
>   my soul

Slipped down to Hell, Hell were a paradise
Whilst thou art here.   [*Exit* GUINEVERE.

> *Mord.*   By Heaven, then thou shalt die!

Enter MORGAN.

Morg. Ryons is trapped, and dying hath confessed
His treason and thine own.

> *Mord.*   Then Arthur lives,

And all is lost.

> *Morg.*   Nay, all is left to win;

This news is secret, and long ere 'tis known
Thy sword shall pierce his heart.

> *Mord.*   Or his sword mine.

> *Morg.* What, wouldst thou question Fate?

> > He Pendragon's son shall slay,
> > That is born with the May.

> > > So Fate decreed:

His blood is thine and mine.

> [*Shouts " Long live King Mordred! Death*
> *to Guinevere!" grow louder to the end.*

> > Go, take thy crown,

And none shall dare to question what is done,
Or what remains to do.   [*Exit.*

   Mord.   So Fate take all!
To halt were death, and that on-coming flood
Of Time's uplifted wave can hold no more.   [*Exit.*

SCENE 2. *The Great Hall at Camelot.*
   *As the scene is disclosed the Hall is filled with
armed* Knights. MORDRED *is on the throne,
accompanied by* MORGAN, *and surrounded by the
retinue of the court.*

   GUINEVERE *stands before the throne.* MORDRED
turns to her.

Y England's knights in council thou dost stand
   Condemned of treason 'gainst thy lord the
       King,
Whose death lies at thy charge. Yet we, who bear
The crown that Arthur wore, now give thee leave
To plead in thy defence. If there be aught
Which thou canst urge why judgment should be
   stayed,
Stand forth and speak.

   Agra.   We pray you hear her not.

   Guin. [*Turning with a look of scorn towards*
   MORDRED.] What still is left to say is not for
   thee!

   Mord. Then let the sentence go. Queen Guinevere,
Daughter of Leodograunce of Cornwall,
Now hear thy judgment as the law decrees :
That first, despoilèd of thy royal robes,
Thou shalt be fastened to an iron stake
Until thy mortal body be consumed
In fiery flames.

   Guin.   And saith the law no more?

Mord. Ay, this it adds : that if thy prayer may
win
Some champion for thy cause, then this same
knight
Shall claim due right of battle 'gainst that lord
Whose charge hath brought thee here.
 Guin.   And who is that ?
 Mord. 'Tis I who charge thee now.
 Guin.   Why then, sir knights,
I'll kneel and pray to you, if haply one
Find heart to serve his Queen.   Think not I plead
For this poor gift of life.   Nay, could I choose,
These hands should bear fresh faggots to the blaze
That lights me to a tomb.   Yet hear me all :
Who stands my knight to-day shall wrest from
  Time
A crown of glory.   Not, sirs, that he fought
For one whose sin knows no desert save death,
That were but shame : yet whoso dares that shame
His sword shall win the right, denied him else,
To slay that crawling thing upon the throne—
Wherefore I cry a champion for my cause !
   [MORDRED, *who has descended from the*
    throne, whispers aside.
 Mord. Too late, my Queen ! too late !   What
  wouldst thou give
To win a king's kiss now ?
      Doth no one speak ?
Then, herald, let the trumpet's tongue bray out !
Her knight is gone a-hawking, or perchance
He sleeps too late !
   [*The trumpet sounds, and at the third call*
    SIR BEDEVERE *breaks through the throng*
    and stands before MORDRED.
 Bed. Hold there, sir herald, hither comes a knight
To answer for the Queen.
 Mord.   Who is this knight ?
 Bed. Sir, by your leave that shall be better told
When all is done.

[*The* Knights *give way, and* ARTHUR *stands*
alone with lowered helm.

Mord.   See, madam, where he stands,
Thy champion, who must needs have come from far
To answer in such cause.

[GUINEVERE *kneels at* ARTHUR'S *feet.*

Guin.   I thank thee, sir ;
Yet now I do repent me of what's done,
And fain would set thee free.   Put up thy sword !
I am not worthy that a true knight's blood
Should flow for me.   See, I will tell thee all :
I had a champion once, the mightiest knight,
The bravest and the truest in the world.
He was my lord, and I his chosen Queen
Brought him to shame.   Then wherefore praise him
     now ?
Nay, sir, I must : for that is life's hard law,
Which will not yield its secret till the close.
When Arthur went the sun shot scarlet-red,
And all the past lay bare.   Then pray thee, sir,
Put up thy sword that waits a worthier cause.

[*A pause, but* ARTHUR *makes no sign.*

Guin. [*To* ARTHUR.] Thou wilt not ?   Then I'll ask
     this much of thee :
When death shall call thee home, it so may chance
That thou shalt meet my lord ; if that should be,
Give him this word,—that at the end, his Queen
Knew him for what he was, true lord of all.

Mord. Go, lead her hence.

Agra.   So God defend our King.

[*Exit* GUINEVERE, *followed by* AGRA-
VAINE *and* Knights.   MORDRED *turns*
to ARTHUR, *who remains motionless,*
MORGAN *watching him intently from*
the steps of the throne.   SIR BEDEVERE
stands by ARTHUR.

Mord. And now I'm thine : yet first, by Heaven,
     I'll know
The face beneath that mask.

Arth.   'Twas kept for thee.
[*As he lifts his helm* MORDRED *starts back.*
Mord. The King.

Arth.   Ay, sir, the King, who but to win
This little hour from out the wreck of time,
Would take life's wearied hand and travel back
Across the ruined past, should fate declare
That only so his sword might claim the right
To slay thee now.

Mord.   Prate on, I fear thee not.

Morg. Thou hast forgot the message of the May ;
Then hear it now.

Arth.   Enough ; 'twas thou, false witch,
That stole the scabbard of Excalibur !
Yet see, the blade remains whose every stroke
Is winged by Death.

Morg.   Not so ! Not so, my lord !
That fickle steel shall splinter as it falls
On one twice armed by fate—

                  " He Pendragon's son shall slay
                  That is born with the May."

                              See ! there he stands !

Arth. Why then the end is here : set on, Sir Knight,
Death stands betwixt us twain, and Death shall
        choose.   [*They fight and* ARTHUR *is wounded.*
Traitor, that blow ends all.   [*He falls to the earth.*

Morg.   Long live the King !
                    [*The trumpet is heard without.*
Dost hear that sound ? Nay, look not on what's
        done,
There's more to do : her soul shall join with his
To wing its way across night's starless sky.
            [*Exeunt* MORGAN *and* MORDRED, *and as
                they go they are greeted by cries from
                without.*

Voices. [*Without.*] Long live the King !

Arth.   Nay, sirs, 'tis not for long.
I'm dying, Bedevere. Where is my sword ?

Bed. There, in thy hand.

Arth. Poor hand, that knew it not.
Go quickly, Bedevere, and bear it hence
Unto that little bay hid in the cliff,
Then cast it in the sea, to wait that day
When upward from the shrieking waves shall spring
A vast sea-brood of mightier strain than ours,
Bearing across the world from end to end
One cry to all, " Our sword is in the sea ! "

Bed. Why, then, 'tis done.

> [*He takes sword, and goes off.*

Arth. Life's tide is ebbing fast.

GAWAINE *enters hurriedly.*

Gaw. Nay, what is here ? The wreck of all the
  world !

Arth. Peace, sir ! I know thy news: the Queen is dead.

Gaw. Not so ; she lives, and thou art well avenged
By one who, dying, struck thy murderer down.

Arth. Didst know him, Gawaine?

Gaw. Ay, I knew him once.
The courtliest knight that ever bare a shield,
The sternest soldier to his mortal foe,
Yet gentlest of us all.

Arth. Nay, sir, his name ?

Gaw. His name, my lord, was Lancelot.

Arth. Lancelot. Ah !
So life's long night is breaking at the last.

> [GUINEVERE *enters, while the figure of*
> MERLIN *appears standing above the*
> *recumbent form of* ARTHUR.

Guin. Where is that knight who died that I might
  live ?

Gaw. Hush, lady ! he is here.

> [*She sees the face of* ARTHUR *and falls at*
> *his feet.*

Guin. My lord ! my lord !

F

Arth. Whose face was there? I pray you, some
  one say,
For all grows dark : I know not where I am.
  Guin. Her name was Guinevere.
  Arth. What, sirs? why then,
This should be Cameliard.
  [*Rousing himself with sudden energy.*
  See, 'tis the spring !
Down in the vale the blossoms of the May
Are swinging in the sun ! and there she stands
That shall be England's Queen !
  Far up I hear
The ceaseless beating of Death's restless wing,
And round mine eyes the circling veil of night
Grows deeper as it falls. Henceforth my sword
Rests in its scabbard. What remains is peace.
  [*He falls back dead.*
  Guin. He's gone, the light of all the world lies dead.
  [*The stage darkens, leaving a light only on the
    face of* MERLIN.
Mer. Not so ; he doth but pass who cannot die,
The King that was, the King that yet shall be ;
Whose spirit, borne along from age to age,
Is England's to the end. Look where the dawn
Sweeps through a wider heaven, and on its wings
By those three Queens of night his barge is borne
To that sweet Isle of Avalon whose sleep
Can heal all earthly wounds.
  [*During this speech the stage grows darker,
    and as the vision appears, at the back, of
    ARTHUR borne in the barge, with the
    three Queens bending over his body, the
    chorus breaks out, and continues till the end.*

CHORUS.

Sleep! oh sleep! till night outworn
Wakens to the echoing horn
That shall greet thee King new-born,
  King that was, and is to be.

And a voice from shore to shore
Cries, " Arise, and sleep no more ;
Greet the dawn, the night is o'er,
   England's sword is in the sea ! "

www.ingramcontent.com/pod-product-compliance
Lightning Source LLC
Chambersburg PA
CBHW030017030726
47499CB00008B/3034